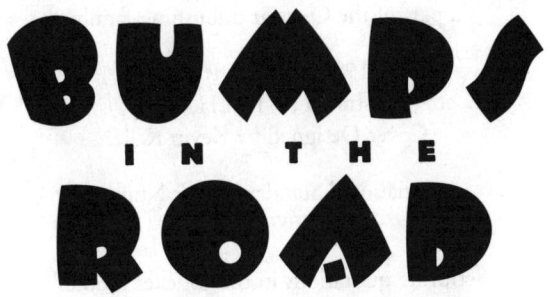

BUMPS IN THE ROAD

A Kids' Bible Study on Overcoming Obstacles

PAULA RINEHART

Gold 'n' Honey Books

Bumps in the Road

published by *Gold 'n' Honey Books*
a part of the Questar publishing family

© 1996 by Paula Rinehart
Illustrated by Tim Haggerty
Cover Designed by Kevin Keller

International Standard Book Number:
1-57673-009-3

Scripture quotations in the "Sticker Studies"
Bible study series for kids are from:
The Holy Bible,
New International Version (NIV)
© 1973, 1984 by International Bible Society,
used by permission of
Zondervan Publishing House;
New American Standard Bible (NASB),
© 1960, 1977 by the Lockman Foundation;
and The Living Bible (TLB),
© 1971 by Tyndale House Publishers

Printed in the United States of America

For information:
Questar Publishers, Inc.
Post Office Box 1720
Sisters, Oregon 97759

96 97 98 99 00 01 02 03 —

10 9 8 7 6 5 4 3 2 1

CONTENTS

WHEN PAULA RINEHART taught at Pantego Christian Academy in Arlington, Texas, one observation amazed her: as she read and discussed the Bible with her students, she found that they "taught" her almost as much as she taught them. Paula decided that someday she wanted to write a Bible study that would help boys and girls feel confident that they could read and understand the Bible for themselves.

Before she could do that, two exciting events happened: Paula and her husband, Stacy, had two children. Eventually, Allison and Brady became the ages of the children Paula had taught.

In addition to this series of Bible studies for kids, Paula has co-authored *Choices: Finding God's Way in Dating, Sex, Singleness, and Marriage* (NavPress, 1982, 1996) as well as a book on women and stress called *Perfect Every Time* (NavPress 1993). She lives with her husband and two teenagers in Raleigh, North Carolina, where she writes and works as a family counselor.

ACKNOWLEDGMENTS

MANY THANKS to the kids and the staff of Colorado Springs Christian School for their help in field-testing these Bible studies for kids — and to my own children, Allison and Brady, for permitting me to use some of the stories from their own experience here on these pages.

A NOTE TO PARENTS
AND TEACHERS

THIS STUDY can be fun to do with your child or a group of children. And it's important that it be fun. Even if you do this study in a classroom, it should never feel like another class. Everyone's grown up on Sesame Street now! You probably remember someone saying this, and it's true: "It's a sin to bore a child with the Word of God."

This study is the perfect thing to combine with a date at McDonald's. Green, leafy trees in the park provide a great setting for this kind of talking.

When you discuss a scene in the Bible, talk as though both of you were there. You were watching from a nearby hill as young Joseph was led off to Egypt as a slave. You were in the tension-filled room with Daniel as he told his trainer that he would eat vegetables instead of the king's royal food. Your hands were helping to pull in empty nets on Peter's fishing boat after a long night with no catch to show for it. You were there.

Expect some exciting things to happen when you open the Bible with a child. He might just tell you what's really on his mind. And even more exciting — he might share something fresh from the passage that you or I had never noticed.

▼ Each Picture Sticker has a different picture on it.
In each chapter you will find a Picture Sticker question.
You'll be asked to find the sticker find the Picture Sticker
with the right picture to help answer that question.

▼ All of the Explore Stickers have a magnifying glass
on them. These stickers go with the questions called
"More to Explore." Each time you finish answering
one of them, place one of these stickers beside it.

▼ Each Message Sticker has different writing on it.
These stickers go with the questions called "Perfect
Fit," which give you important messages to remember.
You have to find the right Message Sticker to complete
the message.

▼ All of the SUPER Question Stickers have a big question
mark on them. After you've answered the study questions
in each chapter, put one of these stickers by your favorite
question.

▼ All of the Prayer Stickers have praying hands on them.
Use one of these stickers after finishing everything else
in each chapter. Stick one by something in each chapter
which you would most like to talk with God about.
Then take a moment to talk with God about this in
your own words. God will listen!

New Confidence

YEARS AGO I was interviewing a man named John Perkins to write a magazine article about his life story. I took a few notes as he talked. But soon I just put down my pencil and listened. I could hardly believe how much this man had lived through!

John grew up as a black man in the Deep South of our country, at a time when prejudice and hardship were part of the very air he breathed. His father left the family when John was just a small boy. He remembers following his father down a path, begging him to stay. John never got to attend school beyond the third grade. He took what skills he had learned and taught himself what he needed to know.

He could have grown up to be an angry, bitter man. But he came to know Christ, and Christ changed his life. Even though John had a secure job and a promising future in California, he knew God was calling him to go back to Mississippi and help his people there. So John went. He felt that God wanted him to help people rebuild their communities according to Christian principles. But John ran into a lot of opposition. Once he was beaten so badly by white police officers that he wasn't sure he would live.

I asked Mr. Perkins how he had the strength to continue in the face of such opposition, with one problem after another coming his way. He seemed surprised that I asked. "Oh," he said, "I've never looked at problems as being permanent or anything. They're just bumps in the road to where I was going."

I have never forgotten those words. They have encouraged me many times through the years as I've been tempted to look at some problem and get discouraged. I know Mr. Perkins is right. With Christ, any difficulty you and I come up against is just a bump in the road to where God is taking us. And that's worth hanging in there for.

As you read the stories of kids in this book who encountered all kinds of different "bumps," and as you look at some of the stories from Jesus' life, I hope you will gain new confidence — Mr. Perkins' kind of confidence — that whatever problem you're facing is, after all, just a "bump in the road" to where you're going.

CHAPTER 1

What If I Don't Have
What It Takes?

MRS. RANDOLPH looked out across her class. "Who can go to the board and work this new math problem?"

A dozen hands shot into the air. Half the class seemed to be jumping out of their seats, hoping for the chance to show off what they knew.

But not Bart. He kept looking down into his open book so the teacher wouldn't call on him.

Maybe she hadn't figured out how lost he felt in her class. Math had never been his strong suit. And in the country school he attended before his family moved away from their ranch this year, they never did problems like these. Percentages, square roots, decimals — they might as well be speaking Greek. Bart wasn't sure he would ever catch up.

Bart's father had encouraged him to talk with his teacher: "Tell her you need extra help. That's what she's there for." But Bart couldn't bear to admit how far behind he was.

Actually, math was only one of the ways Bart felt different from these kids. Sure he could rope a calf and he knew how to plant a garden with a row so straight you'd think he had measured each inch. But these kids didn't care about that. They had all these cool clothes. They had been to exotic places. Every time he stacked up his life with theirs, he seemed to come out on the short end. There were a lot of days when he felt he had the word "Country" tattooed on his forehead. He just wasn't sure he had what it took to be a city kid.

■　■　■

HAVE YOU EVER found yourself in a situation where you didn't know if you had what it took? Maybe you didn't make the team, or you didn't pass the test. Maybe someone needed to hear encouraging words — and you had none. Perhaps someone you cared for had a big financial need — and the money you'd saved was nowhere near enough.

Life is full of situations that cause us to feel hopelessly inadequate. We feel we may as well give up. But if we come to that conclusion, then we haven't looked far enough. God specializes in coming through when we have nowhere else to turn.

There's a familiar story in the New Testament that takes place on a hillside in Galilee. Jesus had just finished speaking. Multitudes of people had been listening to him. Now everyone was hungry. There was no McDonald's on the corner, but then nobody had enough money to buy lunch anyway.

Read for yourself what happened in John 6:1-14.

1 In verses 5-6, Jesus turns to Philip, one of His disciples, and asks this question: "Where are you going to buy bread to feed all these people?" Read verse 7. Did Philip see a solution or just a bigger problem? How did Philip think these people could be fed?

2 Andrew noticed that a boy in the crowd had five barley loaves and two dried fish. How do you think the boy got those, and what were they for?

3 Jesus had everyone sit down. He took the lunch the boy had provided and, after giving thanks, He passed it around to everyone. Put a check by the following statement which correctly states what happened next:
a. Jesus said to everyone, "Be careful to take only one piece of bread and one piece of fish when the basket comes to you. We don't want to run out of food."
b. They all ate as much as they wanted, and there was still food left over.
Select your answer, then find the right Picture Sticker that goes with it.

4 (a.) How many baskets of food were left over?

(b.) What do you think the boy who had given his lunch thought and felt that day?

5 How did the crowds respond after seeing the miracle Jesus performed? (verse 14)

6   This story is found in each of the four Gospels. But only Mark tells how Jesus felt as He earlier looked out on the multitudes that day and began teaching them. Read Mark 6:33-34. How did Jesus feel about these people? *Add an Explore Sticker after you've answered the question.*

Y O U R   T U R N

7   The boy in this story gave up what he had to Jesus… and Jesus took what the boy provided and made it enough for everyone.

(a.) Pick one area in your life where you don't feel as if you have "what it takes." Spend a moment in prayer about this. Imagine yourself giving up your feeling of "not having enough" to the Lord, and ask Him in His own way to give you back what you need. Write out here a sentence of two of your prayer:

(b.) Think back to the scene that began this chapter. What should Bart do about the inadequacy he feels in his new school? What would you tell Bart?

P E R F E C T   F I T

8   Complete this sentence with the right Message Sticker:
     If you bring God what you have…

Next put a Super Question Sticker by your favorite question in this chapter — the one whose answer means the most to you.

THE APOSTLE PAUL was a strong man with a brilliant mind. People listened to him and followed him. But Paul didn't describe himself as brilliant and strong. Listen to what he told the Corinthians:

> You'll remember, friends, that when I first came to you... I didn't try to impress you with polished speeches and the latest philosophy. I deliberately kept it plain and simple: first Jesus and who he is; then Jesus and what he did. I was unsure of how to go about this and felt totally inadequate — I was scared to death, if you want the truth of it.... (1 Corinthians 2:1-5, *The Message*).

That's a picture of Paul with his knees knocking! Sure, Paul knew he was doing what God wanted him to do — telling people about Christ. But Paul wasn't beyond feeling scared and inadequate. He always knew he was just an ordinary person through whom God had chosen to tell His message.

Paul seemed to accept that feeling inadequate is normal. He must have often said to himself, "I don't feel quite able to tackle this." Yet he never let such a feeling stop him. He knew that *God* was able. God could do it. God had called him to this task, and that gave Paul enough courage to go forward — even with his knees knocking!

THE ME I WANT TO BE:

CONFIDENT

WHEN MOST PEOPLE have confidence, it's for obvious reasons. They're confident because they have some special talent that everyone notices, or know the right people, or they they've been to the right places. They have what it takes.

But for a deeper and lasting confidence, God puts the emphasis somewhere else. He says that if our confidence is *in Him* — and in the fact that He lives within us — then no matter how insecure we may feel, or what kind of talents we might be missing, everything will be okay. He's the only real reason for lasting confidence.

Trust in the Lord with all your heart
and do not lean on your own understanding.
(PROVERBS 3:5)

Put a Prayer Sticker by something in this chapter that you would most like to talk with God about. It could be something to thank Him for, or something to ask for His help on. Take a moment just to talk with Him about this, in your own words. God will listen!

CHAPTER 2

No One Understands

SUSAN POUNDED the chalk erasers against the hot sidewalk, just as her teacher had sent her here to do. But she pounded them a little harder than usual. Wham! Chalk dust flew everywhere. Every time she thought of Melinda and Frances, it made her mad.

They were supposed to be her best friends. At least that's what they said. But more and more Susan caught them snickering behind her back.

Today she'd overheard Melinda call her a teacher's pet. "Susan gets picked to do everything," she complained.

A couple of times at the lunch table this week Susan noticed that Frances saved only one seat — for Melinda. Susan had to find a seat on her own. That was a real change. For months they had done everything as a threesome. Now she felt she was being shoved out.

"Can I help it if the teacher always calls on me?" Susan wondered. What was she supposed to do, anyway? Susan liked to be responsible. The teacher knew she could count on her. But it sure made life complicated. She didn't like feeling that her friends were jealous of her.

It all seemed so upside down. "I didn't know you could get into trouble for doing the right thing," she thought to herself.

■　■　■

IF WE'VE DONE something wrong, none of us is too surprised when the roof comes crashing down on our heads. But it's a shock when you do the right thing and then suffer for it.

In the story you're about to read, Jesus healed a man with a withered hand. But He healed him on the Sabbath, which was supposed to be a day of rest, according to the Jewish law.

On the scene that day was a group of Jewish leaders known as the scribes (teachers of the law) and Pharisees. They were important men who liked to show off their importance. They added all sorts of picky rules to God's laws about keeping the Sabbath.

What Jesus did made the scribes and Pharisees furious. They cared more about their own rules than about seeing someone healed.

Turn to Luke 6:6-11. As you read this passage, imagine yourself sitting in a synagogue listening to Jesus teach. Everyone is glancing around nervously. They're watching to see what will happen to a man whose hand hangs limply at his side. What will Jesus do? And how will the Pharisees react?

1   Verse 7 says that the Pharisees were watching closely to see if Jesus healed someone on the Sabbath day. How do you think they wanted to use that against Him?

2   Now think about the other person everyone was watching — the man whose right hand was withered. Imagine how big of a problem his withered hand was in his work and everyday life. What kinds of things might this man be thinking about?

3   No doubt Jesus could have avoided having the Pharisees upset with Him. What are some ways you can think of that He could have kept from angering them?

4   Jesus pointed out that the Sabbath was the best day for doing good (see verse 9). To refuse to do good, when it was within His power to do it, was the same as doing evil. What was "the good" that Jesus intended to do? *Write your answer, then find the right Picture Sticker that goes with it.*

5   Verse 10 says that Jesus singled out this man, then looked at everyone in the crowd before He spoke. Right in front of everyone He said, "Stretch out your hand!" And the man was healed. Can you draw a simple picture that shows what you think this scene looked like? What expressions were on various faces?

6   Everyone in the crowd was probably thrilled by what happened — except the scribes and Pharisees (see verse 11). What kind of plans do you think they were thinking of?

MORE TO EXPLORE

7   Look at Luke 6:5, which records a statement Jesus
    made on another occasion when he offended the
    Pharisees by His actions on the Sabbath. What do
    you think His statement here means?
    Add an Explore Sticker after you've answered the question.

YOUR TURN

8   (a.) Think of an occasion when something bad hap-
    pened to you as a result of something you did right.
    How did you respond?

    (b.) Think again of the scene at the beginning of this
    chapter. What advice would you give to Susan?

9   Complete this sentence with the right Message Sticker:
Even Jesus had to face...

Next put a Super Question Sticker by your favorite question in this chapter — the one whose answer means the most to you.

WHEN WE THINK OF JESUS walking along the roads of Galilee, we easily imagine throngs of people following Him, hanging on His every word. So many people wanted to touch Him, to talk to Him, to be around Him.

But Jesus was not always popular. As long as people thought He would heal their diseases, or give them food, or even save them from the Romans and perhaps become a great King, then the crowds came out. But only a handful of His disciples understood who Jesus really was. Only a few had any inkling that Jesus would be Israel's suffering Savior. By almost everyone else, He was misunderstood.

Hundreds of years before Jesus was born, Isaiah foretold what kind of reception Jesus would receive: "He was despised and rejected by men, a man of sorrows, and familiar with suffering... and we esteemed him not" (Isaiah 53: 3). Isaiah said the suffering Savior would be like someone people hide their faces from.

When we feel we're going through something no one else can understand — when we think no one could feel the way *we* feel — we're in good company. Jesus Himself experienced that feeling. He knew what it means to be misunderstood.

THE ME I WANT TO BE:

PERSEVERING

THINK OF A TIME when you were most tempted to give up. You were tired. You were discouraged. You wondered, "What's the point of going on?" But you kept going. Somewhere deep inside you knew it was important not to give up.

That's called perseverance. Perseverance is the ability to hang in there and keep going even when you don't want to, and no one's giving you any encouragement to.

A mysterious thing happens when you exercise perseverance. You get stronger and stronger. You steadily increase your ability to keep going past the point where others would so easily give up. It's like exercising a muscle until eventually it's strong enough to carry the weight that used to be a strain. Perseverance always builds up to a worthwhile reward.

> **Blessed is the man who perseveres under trial,**
> **because when he has stood the test,**
> **he will receive the crown of life that God**
> **has promised to those who love him.**
> (JAMES 1:12)

Put a Prayer Sticker by something in this chapter that you would most like to talk with God about. It could be something to thank Him for, or something to ask for His help on. Take a moment just to talk with Him about this, in your own words. God will listen!

Needing to Feel Like Somebody

JAKE BUTTONED his jacket as he left the basketball gym. He braced himself for a blast of cold winter air. Scrunch! Scrunch! His new gym shoes made sharply defined tracks in the fresh-fallen snow.

Jake smiled and congratulated himself on his great new shoes. For a moment he imagined himself out-jumping all the other guys on his team.

Then his thoughts came back to reality. He was always looking up to those guys. Being the shortest boy in his class had real disadvantages, especially on the basketball court.

Jake heard someone call his name. "Hey, wait up," Randy yelled. Randy hustled from the gym door to catch up with him. Jake could see from the expression on Randy's face that he was upset.

"What were you doing out there on the court today?" Randy asked, as he came alongside. "You know you can't just keep elbowing like that."

"What's with the lecture?" Jake shot back. "Just because you're bigger than me doesn't mean you know everything!"

Randy only shrugged his shoulders. He wasn't the first person to warn Jake about his attitude.

Jake changed the subject. He knew he couldn't let Randy see him squirm. Yeah, it was true he wasn't supposed to elbow like that, or talk back the way he did all the time. He knew the other guys got tired of his bragging about his new shoes or his dad's sports car or his last trip out west.

But he had to prove he was as good as they were. It was as simple as that.

■   ■   ■

HAVE YOU EVER known someone like Jake — or felt like him yourself?

Jake is a lot like a character in the Bible whose name was Zacchaeus. Zacchaeus spent his life trying to prove he was somebody by pushing other people around, and using his position as a tax collector to cheat them out of their money. But then he met Christ.

To study his story, let's go to the town of Jericho where all those walls came tumbling down many centuries before. Today, Jesus is supposed to be coming through town. Nearly everyone has turned out to see him. And a short guy whom nobody likes has managed to get the best seat in the house.

To read his story, turn to Luke 19:1-10.

1   Look at verses 2 and 3. Some important clues are
    given here about Zacchaeus. What kind of words
    would you use to describe him?
    *Write your answer, then find the right Picture Sticker
    that goes with it.*

2   Why do you think Zacchaeus wanted to see Jesus
    (verse 3)?

3   Jesus looked up to where Zacchaeus was perched, and
    spoke directly to this man whom everyone disliked.
    Think for a minute. What do you think might have
    gone through Zacchaeus's mind after hearing what
    Jesus said to Him?

4   What was everyone's reaction to what Jesus did (verse 7), and why do you think they responded this way?

5   After Jesus and Zacchaeus talked over dinner, Zacchaeus said he would give to the poor half of everything he owned. He also said he would pay back everyone he cheated, and he would pay four times as much as was owed. What do you think caused Zacchaeus to say this?

MORE TO EXPLORE

6   Zacchaeus had spent his whole life trying to be a big shot instead of a small man. Look at what Jesus said in verses 9 and 10. What might Zacchaeus think when he heard what Jesus said? How would Zacchaeus apply these words to himself?
Add an Explore Sticker after you've answered the question.

7   (a.) What kinds of things tend to make you feel "important"?

(b.) Think again about this chapter's opening scene. What is Jake's problem? How can he become confident enough that he doesn't have to be a bully or a big shot to feel like a somebody?

P E R F E C T   F I T

8   Complete this sentence with the right Message Sticker:
Only Jesus can...

Next put a Super Question Sticker by your favorite question in this chapter.

THE PHARISEES were known for wanting to be "big shots." They were the most respected Jewish teachers of the day. Their opinions were the ones that mattered most. When they came into a room, they expected to be given a place of honor. They liked to be called "Rabbi" (which means "Teacher"). They wore special clothing so everyone would notice them as they walked past. They prayed long prayers out loud, just to draw attention to themselves.

The Pharisees were supposed to be religious leaders who represented God. They were supposed to be examples for others to follow. That's why Jesus' disciples were amazed when He told them, "Don't be like the Pharisees...."

Christ called the Pharisees names that must have shocked the ears of everyone who heard. He called them "blind guides" and "fools" and "white-washed tombs," and worst of all, "hypocrites." He told people to listen and follow the Pharisees' words, but not to copy their actions. In other words, the Pharisees were quick to tell others to do things that they, themselves, did not do.

The Pharisees are an example of what happens when a person craves honor and recognition as a "big shot." But in the end, it's not honor that comes to such a person, but rather dishonor and disrespect.

THE ME I WANT TO BE:

A PERSON OF INTEGRITY

INTEGRITY is a word about having a correct fit. Integrity means there's a match between what you appear to be and what you really are. Integrity means there's a perfect connection between what you say you'll do and what you actually do. You could say that integrity was the character quality that the Pharisees were missing most, and that's why Jesus criticized them so severely.

Someone with integrity has a life that backs up his words. What he says is what he does. A person with integrity is the same way in public that he or she is when alone. Having integrity is another way of saying, "I'm for real."

> Search me, O God, and know my heart;
> Try me and know my anxious thoughts;
> And see if there be any hurtful way in me,
> And lead me in the way everlasting.
> (PSALM 139: 23-24)

Put a Prayer Sticker by something in this chapter that you would most like to talk with God about. It could be something to thank Him for, or something to ask for His help on. Take a moment just to talk with Him about this, in your own words. God will listen!

CHAPTER 4

When Parents Argue

MEGAN STUFFED her head under her pillow to block out the noise. Her parents were arguing — again. The sound of their heated words made her stomach tighten into little knots. She wished she had the nerve to tiptoe downstairs and say, "Please stop it, you two!" But deep down she knew this was *their* argument, *their* problem to work out.

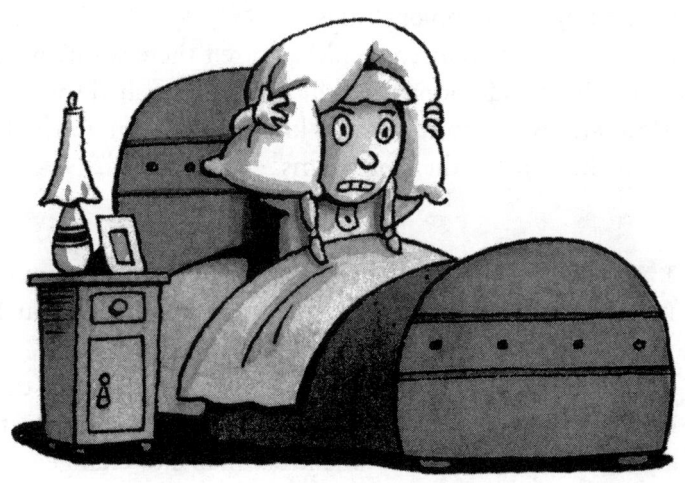

Megan thought her parents loved each other. But that didn't make it any easier to hear them yell at each other when they got upset.

Megan's closest friend, Sarah, had parents who recently divorced. Sarah saw her dad on weekends and stayed with her mother during the week. Megan knew this had been a hard adjustment for Sarah. Megan tried to encourage Sarah. But Megan was scared, too, and hoping that the same thing didn't happen to her family.

Megan lay very still on her bed, trying to block out the sound of her parents' voices. She had her own ways of tuning out their arguments. "Let's see, I have that book report due on Thursday, Sarah's coming to spend the night this weekend, I need to get a present for Dad's birthday...." She had to focus on other things — happier things.

But it was hard. Sometimes Megan felt there wasn't much in her life she could count on right now. She wished she could fall asleep and wake up tomorrow knowing her parents had finally worked out all their problems.

■　■　■

HAVE YOU EVER faced a situation that kept you feeling anxious about the future? Maybe you (like Megan) couldn't do much about it — but you couldn't stop worrying, either!

When you're young, it seems like grown-ups have all the power. They do whatever they want. They don't seem to get stuck just watching from the sidelines, unable to change things. *But that's not true.* Everybody has problems that can't be fixed easily — at least, not overnight, anyway. Everyone has times of feeling powerless. It's easy then to start to worry. But worrying is the opposite of trusting God.

God asks all of us — both kids and grown-ups — to trust Him. He wants us to trust Him even when we can't see what's up ahead, and we're terribly tempted to give in to worry.

Some of Jesus' most treasured words are about not worrying. Turn to Matthew 6:25-34 and read them carefully.

1   (a.) Jesus says we are not to worry about even the most basic things of life. What are those "basic" things He wants us to trust Him for (verse 25)?
Write your answer, then find the right Picture Sticker that goes with it.

    (b.) What other things in life might you be tempted to worry about?

2   Sometimes we may think God will take care of us only if we are good or if we work hard. The truth is that He takes care of us because we belong to Him. What is God called in verses 26 and 32? How much do you feel you can really trust God in a tough situation?

3   How would you restate verse 27 in your own words?

4   Look again at verse 32. Jesus speaks of the "pagans" or the "Gentiles" — He is referring to people who don't know God. These people frantically go about life trying to get what they need. Jesus says, "Don't be like them." What's different for us? Why do we not *have* to worry?

5   Worrying takes energy, but you can do something better with that energy. Read verse 33. Where does Jesus tell you to invest your time and energy?

6   Verse 34 is the big conclusion. How would you express this verse in your own words?

M O R E   T O   E X P L O R E

7   According to verse 33, what does God promise to those who seek first God's kingdom and His righteousness? What do you think that promise means? *Add an Explore Sticker after you've answered the question.*

8   (a.) Maybe you have some worries that are weighing
     down your mind right now. Make a list here of your
     concerns and worries which you can trust God to take
     care of:

     (b.) Think back to the scene that began this chapter.
     What would you say to encourage Megan as she wor-
     ries about her parents' relationship?

P E R F E C T   F I T

9   Complete this sentence with the right Message
     Sticker:
     The opposite of worrying...

     *Next put a Super Question Sticker by your favorite
     question in this chapter.*

THERE'S ONE PERSON above all in Scripture who is famous for worrying. Her name is Martha. She and her sister Mary and her brother Lazarus were close friends of Jesus. He would stay in their home when he came through the town of Bethany.

No doubt Martha was someone everybody could rely on. She could probably have organized a feast for an army and fed them on matching dishes. But when Jesus came for a visit, the Bible says Martha became distracted with all her serving. Her sister Mary sat at Jesus' feet and listened to Him teach — while Martha felt she was left to do all the work. Not exactly a fair deal, Martha thought.

When she complained to Jesus, He answered, "Martha, Martha, you are worried and troubled about many things." Jesus was sitting right in Martha's midst — what need was there to worry, if He was there?

Jesus knew that worry can ruin even the best of occasions. And when things aren't going the way we like them to, worry only makes them worse.

We, too, have Jesus in our midst. But if we give in to worry, we lose the ability to sense His presence and His peace.

THE ME I WANT TO BE:

PEACEFUL

EVERYONE WANTS PEACE. We even have a sign for it that people all over the world recognize — two fingers spread out.

But Jesus said that the peace He gives is something the world doesn't know about. It's not the peace that comes when your life is going along smoothly. The peace of Christ comes from knowing that no matter what happens *to* you, you are safe and secure in Him. Nothing can change that. Christ Himself has promised to bring you through everything and to give you His peace — the same peace that He experienced in His own trials and struggles here on earth.

Peace I leave with you, My peace I give to you;
not as the world gives do I give to you.
Let not your heart be troubled, neither let it be afraid.
(JOHN 14:27)

Put a Prayer Sticker by something in this chapter that you would most like to talk with God about. It could be something to thank Him for, or something to ask for His help on. Take a moment just to talk with Him about this, in your own words. God will listen!

CHAPTER 5

When Good Friends Make Bad Choices

SINCE FIRST GRADE, Ted and John had hung out with the same group of guys in their neighborhood. They all played football on fall afternoons and swam together on hot, steamy days in the summer. Of course, they had their occasional tense moments, but nothing serious. They knew better than to let any difference of opinion stand in the way of something as important as a game or an outing at the pool.

But something strange had begun to happen to the group as they neared middle school. John was starting to stand out as the group's leader. More and more, he was coming up with wild ideas and getting the rest of them involved — wild ideas that could get you into trouble.

The last time John tried to sneak them all into an R-rated movie, Ted pulled him aside. "What's the deal?" Ted whispered. "You're going to get everyone in hot water."

John nearly laughed in his face. "What's the matter with *you,* Ted?" he said loudly. "Are you still a kid, or what?" The other guys stared at Ted. No one said a word. They knew better than to cross John.

Ted had the feeling he was the only one in the group with the nerve to stand up to John. And that made him more than a little nervous.

■　■　■

WHAT DO YOU DO when a good friend seems determined to make bad choices? You can't change his mind. And you can't make his choices for him.

The hardest test of a friendship is not going along when a friend is heading down the wrong path. It's hard to stand alone — but standing alone is always better than going together in the wrong direction.

The story we'll look at now is about a rich young man who was given a choice by Jesus, but who chose to go his own way instead. There's a lot to be learned here. Read Mark 10:17-27 and see what impresses you in this scene.

1   (a.) What did this man do as he came up to Jesus? (verse 17)

    (b.) What is the question he wanted Jesus to answer?

2   What do you learn about this man from the conversation he has with Jesus in verses 19 and 20?

3   (a) How did Jesus feel about this man? (verse 21)

(b.) Because of how he felt about this man, what did Jesus ask him to do?

(c.) Why do you think Jesus asked him to do this?

4 Look carefully at verses 22 and 23. What do you think he was thinking when he heard what Jesus asked him to do?

5 Good Jews were taught that being rich was a sign of God's blessing. But Jesus told this young man to give away his riches! How did the disciples respond as they heard what Jesus said? (verse 24)
Write your answer, then find the right Picture Sticker that goes with it.

6 How would you restate verse 27 in your own words?

7   At least for now, this man could not do what Jesus asked him to do. Why do you think Jesus didn't therefore take back His requirement, and give the man something easier to do instead?
Add an Explore Sticker after you've answered the question.

Y O U R   T U R N

8   (a.) Have you ever watched a friend go the wrong direction, and had to stand alone? If so, what was it like?

(b.) What do you think makes a person strong enough to follow his or her conscience, and not to just follow the crowd?

(c.) Think again about Ted's situation in this chapter's opening scene. What would you advise him to do next?

PERFECT FIT

9   Complete this sentence with the right Message Sticker:
     Sometimes you have to let friends...

Next put a Super Question Sticker by your favorite question in this chapter — the one whose answer means the most to you.

THE JOKES and mocking remarks must have come every day: "Hey, Noah, why does this barn you're building look so much like a boat?" "What a waste of time!"

Talk about doing something that nobody could understand! When God told Noah to build the ark because a great flood was coming, it had never even rained on the earth. The ark was built because of a threat no one believed was real — except Noah.

Noah was faithful to build the ark, then to gather on board his family and all the animals. He was willing to go ahead with what he believed was right no matter what others thought. In the story of the ark, the Bible keeps saying that Noah did everything "just as the Lord commanded." His faithfulness and courage saved his life, and many other lives as well.

As for Noah's neighbors and friends who surely made fun of him, Noah had to let them make their own choices and then accept the consequences. There must have been times when Noah felt alone. But he didn't let that keep him from doing what he knew was right.

THE ME I WANT TO BE:

TRUTHFUL

SOMETIMES WHEN a carpenter is building a wall, he will take out his "plumb line" and hold it against his work to make sure everything is actually straight. The plumb line gives him a *true* straight line that the carpenter tries to follow.

God's truth, His Word, is our plumb line. We measure what we say and what we do against His Word, to know whether we're living and speaking according to the truth.

None of us is free to decide on our own what truth is — God Himself is truth, and He reveals the truth to us in the Bible. All our lives we must keep learning how to "align" ourselves with His truth.

We must live the truth as well as tell the truth. Both are important parts of being "truthful."

> **Guide me in your truth and teach me,**
> **for you are God my Savior,**
> **and my hope is in you all day long.**
> **(PSALM 25:5)**

Put a Prayer Sticker by something in this chapter that you would most like to talk with God about. It could be something to thank Him for, or something to ask for His help on. Take a moment just to talk with Him about this, in your own words. God will listen!

CHAPTER 6

When Friends Let You Down

WHEN MARIA walked through the door of her new class, she realized quickly that she was the only girl in the class who came from another country.

At first that made Maria special. Everyone was curious about her. Where had she come from? How long had she been here? What kind of foods did her family eat? Maria enjoyed the attention. She felt for a while that she had lots of friends. Some of the girls would compete to see who got to sit beside her.

Rachel and Sarah made a big deal about including her in their group of girls. Maria thought it was wonderful to feel that wherever she was — the lunchroom, the playground, wherever — she could fit in. She'd even thought of asking some of the girls to come home with her. Maybe her home would seem different, and they would like the difference!

But this morning, as Maria hung up her coat, she overheard a conversation between Rachel and Sarah that brought tears to her eyes. Sarah was having a birthday skating party on Friday. "Aren't you inviting Maria?" Rachel had asked.

Sarah shrugged her shoulders and whispered, "No, I don't think so. I'd rather keep it to girls like us. She probably doesn't know how to skate anyway."

■　■　■

WHAT DO YOU DO when you feel betrayed by a friend? That's a pain that hurts deep — especially when you feel, as Maria did, that you're rejected just for being who you are.

Sometimes we don't realize that Jesus Himself experienced every kind of pain we will ever know. It's amazing: God took on a human body and became one of us, allowing Himself to experience every heartache we feel.

The scene you're about to read is one of the most piercing ones in the New Testament. Here Jesus is let down terribly by His friends. He's facing the most difficult moment of His life, and He is all alone.

Read Mark 14:32-42.

1   Jesus took His closest friends, Peter and James and
    John, a little deeper into the Garden of Gethsemane.
    How was Jesus feeling at the time? (verses 33-34)

2   What did Jesus ask His friends to do? (verse 34)

3   The word "Abba" which Jesus used in verse 36 for
    His Father is like our word "Daddy." What was Jesus
    asking His Father to do? (verses 35-36)
    *Write your answer, then find the right Picture Sticker
    that goes with it.*

4 When Jesus went back to find His friends, what were they doing? (verse 37)

5 How many times did Jesus find His friends in this condition? (verse 41)

6 How do you think Jesus felt about what Peter and James and John were doing?

7   Matthew and Luke also tell us about this scene. Read
    Luke 22:43. What did God do for Jesus in His hour
    of need?
    Add an Explore Sticker after you've answered the question.

8   (a.) Think of a time when a friend let you down, or
    you let a friend down. In what ways was this situation
    like the one which Jesus went through?

    (b.) Think back to Maria's situation at the beginning
    of this chapter. What would you like to tell Maria, or
    do for her?

9   Complete this sentence with the right Message Sticker:
     Jesus knows every heartache...

Next put a Super Question Sticker by your favorite question in this chapter — the one whose answer means the most to you.

IT'S UNDERSTANDABLE when your enemies give you a hard time. But when a friend treats you badly — that can be tough to take.

As one of the twelve apostles, Judas was a close companion of Jesus. They had worked together, shared meals, and slept under the same roofs and the same open sky.

But Judas, it seems, had a secret life that hardly anyone knew of. As the money-keeper for the twelve apostles he made a regular practice of taking some of it for himself. Then his itching for money led to the worst crime of all. He sold Jesus for thirty pieces of silver. Perhaps Judas realized that Jesus never would be king in the way Judas had hoped, and would never give Judas a place of worldly honor. Maybe Judas wanted something more from his investment. So he was willing to sell out.

The Bible says that after Jesus was arrested, Judas felt bad and tried to return the money. But the Jewish leaders only scoffed at him. In deep remorse and regret, Judas hanged himself, realizing too late what a terrible thing he had done.

Jesus knew that He would be betrayed. But He still showed His full love to Judas and to all the disciples during all the years that they were together.

WHEN IT COMES to friendship, there is probably no trait more valued than loyalty. Loyalty means hanging in there with someone through thick and thin, no matter what.

Loyalty is at the heart of our relationship with God. He is loyal to us, even when we don't deserve it. He also asks us to be loyal to Him.

And God wants us to be loyal in our other relationships, too. Fair-weather friends are those who stick with each other only when it's convenient, when it feels good. But loyalty means you remain true to someone in the hard times as well.

...there is a friend who sticks closer than a brother.
(PROVERBS 18:24)

Put a Prayer Sticker by something in this chapter that you would most like to talk with God about. It could be something to thank Him for, or something to ask for His help on. Take a moment just to talk with Him about this, in your own words. God will listen!